GIN AUSTEN

Also by COLLEEN MULLANEY

It's Five o'Clock Somewhere

The Stylish Girl's Guide to Fabulous Cocktails

Sparkle & Splash

GIN AUSTEN

50 COCKTAILS

to Celebrate the Novels
of Jane Austen

COLLEEN MULLANEY

Photographs by
Christopher Bain

STERLING EPICURE
New York

STERLING EPICURE
New York

An Imprint of Sterling Publishing Co., Inc.
1166 Avenue of the Americas
New York, NY 10036

ISBN 978-1-4549-3312-0

Distributed in Canada by Sterling Publishing Co., Inc.
ᶜ/o Canadian Manda Group, 664 Annette Street
Toronto, Ontario, M6S 2C8, Canada
Distributed in the United Kingdom by GMC Distribution Services
Castle Place, 166 High Street, Lewes, East Sussex, BN7 1XU, United Kingdom
Distributed in Australia by NewSouth Books
University of New South Wales, Sydney, NSW 2052, Australia

For information about custom editions, special sales, and premium
and corporate purchases, please contact Sterling Special Sales
at 800-805-5489 or specialsales@sterlingpublishing.com.

Manufactured in Canada

2 4 6 8 10 9 7 5 3 1

sterlingpublishing.com

Interior design by Christine Heun
Cover design by Elizabeth Lindy

Wedgewood piece courtesy of Linda Jewett
For Image Credits, see page 133

CONTENTS

INTRODUCTION

"I believe I drank too much wine last night
at Hurstbourne; I know not how else to
account for the shaking of my hand to-day."
—Jane Austen to Cassandra Austen, 1800

orn in 1775, Jane Austen lived during the
late Georgian era and wrote six major novels,
including the literary classics *Sense and Sensibility*
and *Pride and Prejudice*, as well as a handful of other, less
renowned pieces. Not widely read during her lifetime, Austen's
books gained in popularity after her death in 1817, at the age
of 41. The social commentary of her work centers around her
characters' quest for security, love, or both. Austen, like so
many of us, pursued happily ever after in many different
forms and places.

Fret not if you do not know Austen's life or literary universe
well. Her novels blend the details of the life that she led and one
of which she only could dream. We almost can feel the salt air on

the promenade in *Persuasion* or smell the garden roses in *Emma*. We revel in the coziness of the picturesque cottages and admire the grandeur of the majestic estates in each of her stories. Her characters play the pianoforte, visit friends, chat in gardens, and attend dances. She describes these events in detail, effortlessly transporting us into the past. In her way, she shows us how to live a more civilized life and find happiness in everyday moments.

Much of her storytelling takes place at social engagements: picnics, luncheons, dinner parties, and glamorous balls that last well into the night. At these gatherings, gossip reigns, love flourishes, and drinks flow. So let us begin our adventure by raising a glass and making a toast to Miss Austen herself. Make this strong, attractive cocktail—possessed of enough sweetness and just the right amount of acidity—to celebrate the author of the incredible stories that she gave us.

GIN AUSTEN

5 sage leaves
½ ounce lemon juice
2 ounces gin
2 ounces Lillet rosé
1 dash orange bitters

In a mixing glass, muddle four sage leaves with the lemon juice. Add the gin, Lillet rosé, bitters, and ice. Stir well, and strain into a coupe. Garnish with the remaining sage leaf, settle in, and read on.

"The orange wine will
want our care soon.
But in the meantime,
for elegance and ease
and luxury, the Hattons
and Milles dine here
to-day, and I shall eat ice
and drink French wine,
and be above vulgar
economy."

—Jane Austen to Cassandra Austen, 1808

Austen never married. From her letters to her sister, Cassandra, we can surmise that she fell intensely in love once, but the relationship, if indeed one truly existed, ended without a proposal. Many years later, she accepted a proposal of marriage from one Reginald Bigg-Wither—for less than a day, according to one of her nieces—but she swiftly rescinded her acceptance of his offer the following morning.

Despite lacking a husband, Austen had a great deal of love in her life, forming close relationships with her family, friends, and members of her church. Perhaps she found the contentment that she wanted by observing marriage from a distance. Even if she never had her own happy ending, she devoted herself to devising them for her characters and for us, her readers. In that regard, her imagination certainly served her far better than Emma Woodhouse's did for her.

JANE'S ADDICTION

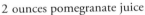

2 ounces gin
2 ounces pomegranate juice
½ ounce lime juice
   sparkling rosé
   raspberries for garnish

Into a shaker filled with ice, pour the gin, pomegranate juice, and lime juice and shake well. Strain into a wine glass, and top with sparkling rosé. Garnish with the raspberries, and ponder Jane's love of love.

George Austen, the family patriarch, died when Jane was 30 years old. A period of domestic turbulence followed, in which the Austen women—Jane, her mother, and sister—moved house frequently. They eventually settled into a cottage owned by Jane's brother Edward. There she focused solely on her writing and, with the assistance of her brother Henry, began seeking publication for her novels. Issued anonymously, her first four books saw critical and some popular success. Her final two novels, written in younger days, appeared posthumously and contained a note revealing her identity and their connection to her previous work. Over the decades and now centuries, these books have taken on lives of their own, all the while retaining their reputation for feisty wit and relatable characters through countless adaptations. So let us raise our glasses again to this fascinating woman who led a remarkable life and created even more remarkable worlds for us to celebrate.

Jane Austen's family home in the Hampshire village of Chawton.

GEORGIAN DRINKS

*L*ike Austen's characters, cocktails possess distinctive personalities: charming, clumsy, complex, crazy, mysterious, seductive, sensual, or witty. Like a good book, a carefully crafted drink has a story to tell and makes for a most marvelous journey.

Harry Croswell, a newspaperman in America, defined the cocktail as we know it in 1806, the same year that Austen's family moved in with her brother Frank in Southampton and a few years before she wrote *Sense and Sensibility*. In response to a reader's question about the unfamiliar word, Croswell described it in the pages of *The Balance and Columbian Repository* of Hudson, New York, thus: "a stimulating liquor, composed of spirits of any kind, sugar, water, and bitters—it is vulgarly called a bittered sling . . . ."

What would Austen's cast of characters have drunk? In her novels and letters, she mentions wine (often mixed with water) and fortified wines such as Port and Madeira, as well as beer, cordials, punch, and rum. At the time, people were just beginning to consume mixed drinks, as we would call them, but a tantalizing world of alcoholic concoctions existed long before then.

FLIPS
This family of cocktails contains an entire egg among its ingredients. It may sound odd at first notion, but these drinks are not as rare as you might think. Eggnog—essentially a flip

plus cream—is a close cousin to the family. The first written evidence of flips dates to the late 1600s and indicated a mixture of rum, ale, molasses, and egg, served hot. It had not changed much by Austen's time.

JULEPS

From the Persian word for "rosewater," this cocktail family originally combined any spirit with fresh mint, an herb used for centuries as as a digestive aid.

PUNCHES

All branches of the cocktail tree descend from the almighty punch, the world's first cocktail. The first known written reference to it, in the hand of a worker for the British East India Company, dates to 1632. A few years later, a German man also stationed in India described the drink as a combination of liquor, rosewater, citrus juice, and sugar. Now shorthand for a large-format party drink, the word "punch" itself derives from the Hindi word *panch*, meaning "five," indicating the five requisite ingredients: spirit, citrus, sugar, water, spice. Experts believe that English sailors created it when their rations of wine and beer either went flat and rancid in the warmer climes of the subcontinent or when they had exhausted their supplies of said rations. In response, they created a sort of artificial wine from the ingredients

Sir John Middleton toasts to Elinor Dashwood's
"best affections" after Edward's visit.
—nineteenth-century illustration from *Sense and Sensibility*

indigenous to their surroundings: rum or arrack, citrus, and spices. The seamen brought the drink with them to London and beyond, and it continued to spread.

SHRUBS

This family of drinks takes its name from its primary flavoring component, a sweetened vinegar-based fruit syrup. Such syrups were and remain an excellent way of preserving fruit long past harvest. With centuries-old roots in the Arabic world, the earliest versions featured citrus juice blended with spices, rose petals, and other flavorings. In the 1700s, Europeans added rum or brandy. Later that century, vinegar largely replaced citrus juice as a preserving agent because it was easier to procure. Today the cocktail combines a spirit, shrub syrup, and water (often carbonated).

SLINGS

As noted, the original definition of the cocktail provides a synonym for the term: "vulgarly called a bittered sling." That description aptly describes the contents of a sling, namely a cocktail without bitters: spirit, sugar, and water only. In modern times, the water usually is carbonated, and ginger ale serves as a common substitute.

SOURS

In this family of drinks, citrus juice—chiefly lemon or lime— takes a lead role, joined by a spirit and sugar or a sweet liqueur.

Historians also believe this cocktail to have naval roots in the eighteenth century. On long sea journeys, sailors had rations of liquor as well as citrus to stave off scurvy. They added the citrus juice to the spirit, usually whiskey or rum, to mask its flavor. Today an egg white occasionally adds texture, such as some renditions of the Whiskey Sour. Modern examples of the sour include the classic Daiquirí or Margarita.

TODDIES

Closely related to to slings, toddies consist of a spirit, sugar or honey, water, and spices, and they frequently (but not always) are served hot. By 1786, that was its official definition. Its origins lie in British-controlled India as well, where a drink made with fermented palm sap, called *tadi*, proved popular among the colonists.

While we take our cues from the drinks of Austen's age, the libations that follow accommodate today's tastes. They have, you might say, a more modern sensibility. As each of the novels has a distinctive setting, so the cocktails follow suit. Whether by the sea, tropically influenced, in a garden of delights, layered and mysterious, or a classic by heart, each has a story to tell. Drink on and find yours.

BARWARE

*L*ike writing a perfectly penned story, the keys to creating a well-crafted cocktail are shaking the components or stirring them in dramatic flair and then straining what is not needed. The proper tools will assist you nobly in your efforts.

BARSPOON
These long-handled spoons, often featuring a spiraled shaft, allow you to crack and shape ice and to stir a cocktail in a mixing glass elegantly.

BLENDER
Use a stick or immersion blender for preparing liquid ingredients and a countertop model for ice.

JIGGER
As in storytelling, precision is essential. Invest in a double-sided jigger with fractions marked inside the measuring cups.

JUICER
Whether you use an electric or a handheld model, fresh juice is essential for adding liveliness and character to a cocktail.

MIXING GLASS

Like a ball, the right atmosphere is crucial for mixing together different components. Use this glass with a spout whenever you need to stir a drink with ice before pouring it into the serving vessel.

MUDDLER

This culinary rod releases the flavor of fruits and herbs.

SHAKERS

Styles include the Boston (a pint glass and a large shaking tin), the most dangerous of the bunch because glass can shatter; the cobbler (with a cap over the strainer, which fits into the bottom tin); the Parisian (two stainless steel tins that join with a clean seam); and, best in show, the weighted shaker, in which a smaller tin fits into a larger tin.

STRAINERS

A Hawthorne strainer—with a flat top, central perforations, and a metal spiral around the edge—fits snugly into the large tin of any shaker and allows you to adjust the straining level by pushing the spiral forward. A julep strainer has a perforated metal bowl with a handle and will fit snugly into a mixing glass to strain stirred drinks. A mesh strainer also proves useful.

Y-SHAPED VEGETABLE PEELER

This design safely allows you to make proper twists for garnishes.

GLASSWARE

Every good home should have a variety of glassware. In Austen's time, proper tabletop etiquette was of paramount importance. Today it still is crucial to have a suitable glass for your drink. But if you do not possess all that follow—or if, as in the case of the Dashwood family, a greedy sister-in-law kept the good crystal—it is perfectly permissible to improvise. Always chill your glassware in advance, and, if a glass has a stem or a handle, hold it by same.

COLLINS GLASS

 This tall, cylindrical glass, named for the Tom Collins cocktail, holds 10 to 14 ounces and preserves carbonation nicely.

COPPER MUG

 These metal cups with handles are the traditional vessels for bucks and mules.

COUPE

 This classic and elegant glass, purportedly modeled on the left breast of Queen Marie Antoinette, typically holds 5 or 6 ounces of craft cocktails not served on ice.

FLUTE

This narrow, stemmed vessel that holds 4 to 7 ounces of liquid preserves carbonation while preventing the drinker's hand from warming the glass.

HIGHBALL GLASS

A rough cross between a Collins and a rocks glass, this 8-ounce glass, named for a piece of railroad equipment indicating the speed at which the drink within could be made, is used generally for drinks with a carbonated component.

HURRICANE GLASS

Named for the glass of a hurricane lamp, which it resembles, hurricane glasses generally hold about 20 ounces and are used for larger-volume tropical drinks. Smaller versions are called "colada" or *poco grande* glasses.

IRISH COFFEE MUG

This glass mug styled with a handle and short-stemmed foot holds 6 to 8 ounces.

JULEP CUP

This conical, footed silver cup has a banded or beaded rim.

LIQUEUR GLASS

Use this 2 to 3 ounce (6–9cl) glass for serving aperitifs and digestifs.

MARGARITA GLASS

A stemmed glass with two bowls of different sizes, this glass serves its namesake drink and other cocktails typically blended with ice.

MARTINI GLASS

This stemmed, V-shaped glass, which evolved from the coupe, habitually serves martinis or other stirred drinks. Smaller iterations of the glass held only 4 ounces. Larger, more modern styles hold up to 8 ounces and prove notoriously unwieldy.

PUNCH GLASS

This glass or crystal mug generally holds 4 to 6 ounces.

ROCKS GLASS

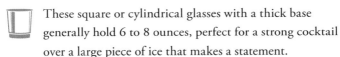 These square or cylindrical glasses with a thick base generally hold 6 to 8 ounces, perfect for a strong cocktail over a large piece of ice that makes a statement.

SHOT GLASS

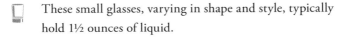 These small glasses, varying in shape and style, typically hold 1½ ounces of liquid.

WINEGLASS

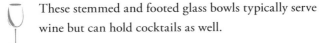 These stemmed and footed glass bowls typically serve wine but can hold cocktails as well.

INGREDIENTS

The main characters in a cocktail determine the tale told, whether in a book or in your glass.

BITTERS
In Austen's day, bitters were medicinal, containing herbs and other botanicals steeped in alcohol and used to treat a variety of ailments. Their formulations have changed little in the intervening centuries, although now they primarily add flavor and depth to a cocktail. If a recipe calls for a specific brand, such as Angostura or Peychaud's, that distinct type proves integral to the taste of the finished drink. Experimentation is encouraged, however, since, as Austen well knew, variety is indeed the spice of life.

CARBONATION
Bubbles render a drink festive. Always add carbonated ingredients—club soda, ginger ale, sparkling wine, or the like—*after* you have poured the drink into the serving glass, and do not shake or stir it vigorously afterward!

CITRUS
Freshly squeezed juice is essential for quality cocktails. Even if you cannot do as Mr. Knightley does and pluck limes from your own trees, it is worth a trip to the store for fresh fruit. Never use prepackaged juices! Doing so would be most improper.

Mr. Knightly expresses his devotion to Emma Woodhouse.
—nineteenth-century illustration from *Emma*

EGGS

If you want to do it as they would have in Austen's day, select small, organic eggs, coddle them briefly in 90 to 120°F water, and then dry them immediately. Otherwise, it is far easier to use packaged, pasteurized egg whites.

GARNISHES

Select only the freshest fruits and herbs for garnishes. Mint, for instance, wilts quickly at room temperature. When making citrus twists, use a Y-shaped peeler and avoid the pith, which, like an unwanted relative, will add undesirable bitterness to the mix. Hold the length of peel, skin side down, over the drink, and twist it firmly to express its oils. Rub it around the rim of the glass, and then float it, skin side up, in the drink. Cherries used as garnishes should be brandied cherries or cocktail cherries. When using grated spices such as cinnamon or nutmeg, always rasp them freshly to optimize their aromatics.

ICE

Good quality ice helps achieve a properly chilled and diluted cocktail. When shaking a drink, use crushed ice, which you can make by placing ice cubes into a clean plastic bag and crushing them with a rolling pin or meat tenderizer. When serving a drink on the rocks, always build the complete drink first and add the ice last, immediately before serving—unless instructed otherwise.

LIQUEURS

Made from a base spirit infused with flavorings such as flowers, fruits, or herbs, liqueurs typically taste sweet and strong. Recipes in this book call for Grand Marnier, St. Germain, and crème de violette among others.

SPIRITS

BRANDY comes in two major categories. Eaux de vie refers to a distilled spirit made from various fruits such as apples, apricots, pears, or the like. Producers make traditional brandy by distilling wine and then aging it. Armagnac and cognac brandies come from specific regions of France. Italy produces grappa, and Chile makes pisco. If a recipe does not name a kind or style of brandy, you cannot go wrong with a good cognac.

GIN consists of a neutral grain base flavored with juniper, coriander, and often dozens of other botanicals. Among their number, cassia bark and licorice are thought to function as stimulants, possibly even providing a clarion call—necessary, at times, to recognize what's been in front of you all along. Plymouth and Old Tom styles taste sweeter, whereas London Dry and Dry taste less so. When a recipe does not call for a specific style, use London Dry.

MEZCAL, from a Nahuatl phrase meaning "oven-cooked agave," comes from the agave plant. Any country can produce mezcal, which possesses a smoky taste, although agave grows chiefly in Mexico. Tequila is a kind of mezcal made exclusively from the blue agave plant and around the city of Tequila in Mexico. Most tequila used in cocktails is of the unaged white or silver (*blanco* or *plata*) classification. For sipping neat, you may prefer the "rested" *reposado* style, aged for at least two months, or the *añejo* classifcation, aged for at least a year.

RUM derives from molasses, a by-product of transforming sugarcane into sugar, primarily in the Caribbean—where Sir Thomas of *Mansfield Park* had his plantation. Extremely diverse, the spirit has three main styles: English, big and bold, produced in Barbados, Jamaica, the Virgin Islands, and other formerly English colonies; French, grassy and herbal and called *Rhum Agricole*, from Guadeloupe, Haiti, Martinique, and other formerly French colonies; and Spanish, more delicately flavored and called *Ron*, made in Cuba, Guatemala, Nicaragua, and other formerly Spanish colonies. Cachaça, a sugarcane-based cousin to rum, hails from Brazil.

VODKA, a colorless, odorless, tasteless spirit by law, is distilled from grains or potatoes.

WHISKEY, in addition to blends from Canada, Ireland, and Japan, also encompasses bourbon (American), rye, and scotch (Scottish). The spirit's wide range of flavors results from the use of different grains and various methods of distilling.

SYRUPS
See page 24 for the recipes used in this book.

VERMOUTH
This category of fortified wine comes in two main styles: dry (white and primarily French) and sweet (red and generally Italian).

Sir Thomas presents Henry Crawford to Fanny Price.
—nineteenth-century illustration from *Mansfield Park*

SYRUPS

Not just mere sweeteners, these sweet solutions add body and flavor to cocktails, often tempering the intensity of stronger ingredients.

EARL GREY SYRUP

1 cup sugar
1 cup water
4 Earl Grey tea bags

In a saucepan over medium heat, combine all ingredients and stir until the sugar dissolves. Remove from heat, and let tea steep for 10 to 15 minutes. Remove the tea bags, pour the syrup into an airtight container, and store in the refrigerator for up to two weeks.

GRENADINE

1½ cups pomegranate juice
1 cup sugar
juice of half a lemon

In a saucepan over medium heat, combine the pomegranate juice and sugar, stirring until the sugar dissolves. Reduce heat to low, and stir until the mixture thickens. Remove from heat, and add the lemon juice. Cool and store in an airtight container in the refrigerator for up to two weeks.

HIBISCUS SYRUP

1 cup sugar
2 cups water
¾ cup dried hibiscus leaves
2 star anise
1 teaspoon grated ginger
 juice of half a lemon

In a saucepan, combine the sugar and water and bring to a boil. Stir until the sugar dissolves; then remove from heat. Add the hibiscus leaves, star anise, and ginger, and allow the mixture to steep for up to 30 minutes. Add the lemon juice, stir to combine, and strain through a mesh strainer into an airtight container. The syrup will keep in the refrigerator for up to two weeks.

LAVENDER SYRUP

1 cup sugar
1 cup water
3 tablespoons edible lavender blossoms

In a saucepan, boil the sugar and water until the sugar dissolves. Add the lavender, remove from heat, and let steep for 20 minutes. Strain the syrup into an airtight container, and store for up to two weeks in the refrigerator.

LIME-MINT SYRUP

1 cup sugar

1 cup water

zest of 1 lime

10 to 12 mint leaves

In a saucepan, combine the sugar and water and boil, stirring until the sugar dissolves. Remove the saucepan from the heat, add the lime zest and mint leaves, and let steep for 20 minutes. Strain the mixture into an airtight container, and keep in the refrigerator for up to two weeks.

ORGEAT

¼ pound raw almonds

1 cup water

½ cup white sugar

¼ cup demerara sugar

¼ ounce cognac

¼ teaspoon orange flower water

Preheat the oven to 350°F. In a food processor, carefully grind the almonds to a medium consistency (*not* a paste). Spread them on a baking sheet, and cook for 12 to 15 minutes, until golden. In a small saucepan over medium heat, combine the water, toasted almonds, and both sugars and bring to a boil. Remove from heat, and blend into a paste. Strain the paste through a mesh strainer or cheesecloth. Add the cognac and orange flower water, and stir well. Cool and bottle.

RHUBARB SYRUP

½ cup water
½ cup sugar
2 cups chopped rhubarb

In a saucepan, combine all ingredients and bring to a boil. Reduce heat, simmer for 15 minutes, and remove from heat. Pour the mixture into a food processor or a blender, and blend until smooth. Strain through a mesh strainer or cheesecloth into an airtight container. The syrup will keep for up to two weeks in the refrigerator.

ROSEMARY SYRUP

1 cup water
1 cup sugar
¼ cup rosemary leaves

In a saucepan, combine all ingredients and bring to a boil, stirring constantly until the sugar dissolves. Reduce heat and let simmer for two minutes. Remove from heat and let sit twenty minutes to allow flavors to marry. Strain syrup into an airtight container. Syrup will keep for up to two weeks in the refrigerator.

SIMPLE SYRUP

1 cup water
1 cup sugar

In a saucepan over low heat, combine the ingredients and stir until the sugar dissolves. Cool and bottle in an airtight container. The syrup will keep in the refrigerator for up to three weeks.

METHODS

If something is worth doing, it is worth doing properly. These techniques will achieve all of your cocktail aims correctly.

BLEND
When using a countertop blender, pulse generously to break the ice without breaking the machine. If using a stick or immersion blender, always keep the blades and their protective cover below the surface level of the liquid. Otherwise you will be wearing your cocktail rather than drinking it.

BUILD
Add the ingredients in the order specified directly into the serving vessel.

CHAFE
For hot drinks, fill the serving vessel with hot water to warm it. Discard the water before adding the cocktail.

CHILL
Place serving glassware in the freezer for at least 20 minutes before pouring the cocktail into it. If your freezer does not possess the requisite space, fill each glass with ice and water, set aside for 20 minutes, and discard ice and water before mixing a drink.

FLOAT

Flip a barspoon upside down, place it in the glass near the surface of the liquid, and pour the top layer of the drink slowly over the back of the spoon.

GARNISH

When executed properly, a garnish can turn a workaday drink into a work of art. For twists, use a Y-shaped peeler, making sure to avoid the pith of the citrus. Pinch the twist, skin side down, over the drink, rub it around the rim of the glass, and then float it, skin side up, in the drink. Grate chocolate, cinnamon, nutmeg, and other garnishes fresh for best effect. Also consider fans, spirals, wedges, and wheels for dramatic presentation.

MIX

Fill the mixing glass half full with ice cubes, and stir for a few seconds to chill the glass. Add the specified ingredients, and stir with gusto for 20 seconds before using a julep strainer to strain the drink into the serving vessel.

MEASURE

Accuracy counts. Use a double-sided jigger, and follow measurements precisely.

MUDDLE

Use a muddler to press the juices or oils from fruit or herbs. Crushing or smashing them them will release unwanted bitterness. When muddling herbs such as mint or basil, use only the leaves (no stems).

RIM

Into a shallow dish, pour the rimming ingredient, such as salt or sugar. Wipe a citrus wedge (grapefruit, lemon, lime, or orange, depending on the ingredients of the drink) around the outside edge of the mouth of the serving glass. Invert the glass, and roll only the outside edge in the rimming material. Avoid rimming the inside of the glass, which will alter unconscionably the flavor of the drink.

SHAKE

Fill the shaker half full of ice, and shed your ladylike demeanor when shaking a cocktail, which aerates, chills, and dilutes the finished drink. If using eggs or cream, add them last to avoid curdling. Always ensure your shaker is sealed tightly *before* you perform your exertions. Do it hard and fast—but you need not overdo it. Shaking for more than 20 seconds will bruise or overdilute a drink. Strain shaken drinks with a Hawthorne strainer.

STIR

Prepare stirred cocktails in a mixing glass with plenty of ice, which will chill and dilute them properly. Use a barspoon to stir, and strain through a Julep strainer into the serving vessel.

STRAIN

Use a Hawthorne strainer for shaken drinks, a julep strainer for stirred drinks, and a mesh strainer for drinks shaken with muddled ingredients or egg.

TEST

Press the back of your hand to the side of a glass to determine its approximate temperature. When testing for taste, place a clean straw into the drink, cap the straw with a finger, and release the liquid into your mouth. Never reuse a test straw.

I

SENSE AND
SENSIBILITY

*T*O FIND THE PROPER BALANCE IN LIFE, ought we succumb to impassioned, uncontrolled excesses of sensibility or instead place sense above all else at the risk of becoming passionless and dull? Sisters Elinor and Marianne Dashwood model this timeless dilemma for us to behold. At first glimpse, rational Elinor represents sense, while passionate Marianne embodies sensibility, but each woman harbors more complex feelings than Austen initially leads us to believe. Both Dashwood girls are searching for love, each endeavoring to find it in her own particular way. When circumstance expels them from their home and they go to live in Barton Park, opportunities for romance abound. As in this classic love story, these variations on traditional cocktails prove the value of striking a gratifying compromise between extremes.

"There are two traits in her character which are pleasing,— namely, she admires Camilla, and drinks no cream in her tea."

—Jane Austen on Miss Fletcher
to Cassandra Austen, 1796

DEVONSHIRE DREAMCICLE

AUSTEN ADORED DEVONSHIRE, A PICTURESQUE county in southwest England. In it, she sets Barton Cottage, to which the Dashwood women repair after being cast from Norland, their former home. Austen lovingly describes the natural beauty of the surrounding landscape—lush hills, verdant lawns, rose gardens—with as much care as she does the houses themselves. Devonshire cream, which hails from the county, has a nutty, sweet flavor and creamy texture. The Dashwoods surely enjoyed the thick, clotted cream with tea and scones, and they no doubt would have appreciated this creamy cocktail on a summer afternoon.

> 2 ounces vanilla-flavored vodka
> 1 ounce triple sec
> 2 ounces orange juice
> 1 ounce half and half
> ½ cup ice
> orange for garnish

In a blender, pour all ingredients, blend until smooth, and pour into a margarita glass. Garnish with 1 tablespoon orange zest and an orange slice and dream of an afternoon spent in the rolling English countryside.

TIP Elevate your next afternoon tea or book club gathering with a round of these tempting delights.

HOT BARTON RUM

AFTER THE UNTIMELY DEATH OF HENRY DASHWOOD, John Dashwood—his son by his first marriage—and John's selfish wife, Fanny, inherit Norland, the family house. John and Fanny promptly eject the second Mrs. Dashwood and her daughters—Elinor, Marianne, and Margaret—who had been living there in harmony for many years. The women take refuge at Barton Cottage, which they rent from a considerably kinder relative. Life begins anew. This libation provides liquid insulation from a chilly afternoon or, better yet, from Fanny's cold shoulder. If you should find yourself, like Marianne, running down hills in the pouring rain or heartsick over a rogue who has fled to London to marry a wealthy heiress, it may behoove you to imbibe one.

- ½ cup water
- 1 ounce unsalted butter
- 1 tablespoon honey
- ¼ tablespoon orange zest
- ⅛ teaspoon anise
- ⅛ teaspoon cloves
- ⅛ teaspoon nutmeg
- ½ tablespoon brown sugar
- 1 pinch salt
- 2 ounces spiced rum cinnamon stick for garnish

In a saucepan, bring the water to a boil. Add the butter, honey, orange zest, spices, brown sugar, and salt. Stir continually until the butter melts and the sugar dissolves. Remove from heat, and add the rum. Strain through a mesh strainer into a chafed Irish coffee mug, garnish with a cinnamon stick, and, if a disagreeable relative sends you away, do take the rum with you.

"As a house, Barton Cottage, though small, was comfortable and compact; … from first seeing the place under the advantage of good weather, they received an impression in its favour."

—Jane Austen, *Sense and Sensibility*

JUST A DASHWOOD

WHAT IS A DASH? IT IS A QUANTITY DEEMED acceptable, modest, and proper. Add the right amount, and it renders everything perfect. Add too much, and you've ruined the mix. But what if your dash and another's dash do not align? Within the Dashwood family, for instance, Marianne's dash clearly varies from Elinor's. To add a sufficient quantity of dash is to strike the appropriate balance in life, and the correct amount varies according to one's particular fancy. This cocktail will assist you in finding yours.

2 ounces genever
1 ounce orgeat
1 ounce lemon juice
1 ounce pineapple juice
3 dashes Angostura bitters

In a shaker filled with ice, pour the genever, orgeat, and juices and shake well. Strain into a coupe, and carefully administer the dashes, one for each sister.

VARIATION If you cannot lay hands on genever, substitute a juniper-forward gin.

....

"I wish, as well as everybody else, to be perfectly happy; but, like everybody else, it must be in my own way."

—Elinor Dashwood

....

ELINORANGE BLOSSOM

RATIONAL AND DEPENDABLE, ELINOR IS THE ELDEST
Dashwood daughter and the most mature of her sisters. The
anchor of her family, she exhibits steadfast sense in all she
does and acts as a foil to her sister Marianne's surplus of sensibility. When Elinor learns that Edward, her one true love, had
betrothed himself to another years ago, heartbreak engulfs her,
but she remains strong, despite her aching disappointment. In
the end, her loyalty wins the day, and unfettered love blossoms
between Elinor and Edward.

> 1½ ounces Bombay Sapphire gin
> 1½ ounces sweet vermouth
> 1½ ounces orange juice
> sparkling wine
> orange for garnish (optional)

In a shaker filled with ice, pour the gin, vermouth, and orange
juice, shake well, and strain into a coupe. Top with sparkling
wine, garnish, if you like, with an orange slice, and remember
that true love triumphs in the end.

. . . .

"A glass of wine, which Elinor procured for her
directly, made her more comfortable, and she was at
last able to express some sense of her kindness."
—Jane Austen, *Sense and Sensibilty*

. . . .

BRANDON OLD-FASHIONED

LOYAL, STEADFAST, AND TRUE, COLONEL BRANDON steps in when needed most. He provides an acquaintance with a means to earn a living and prove worthy of a wife; he accepts guardianship over a child who bears no relation to him; and of course he helps his beloved Marianne recover from heartbreak caused by another. Passion guides Marianne more than practicality, so waiting for her to come to her senses is not a task for the faint of heart. A gentleman deserves a refined drink while he holds out hope for the day when his love realizes the place that she occupies in his heart—and he in hers. Enjoy this cocktail with friends who are equally faithful and patient.

    1 orange slice
    1 cocktail cherry
    1 sugar cube or 1 teaspoon granulated sugar
    2 ounces brandy
    3 dashes Angostura bitters
      club soda
      cocktail cherry and orange for garnish

In a rocks glass, muddle the orange slice, cherry, and sugar. Add the brandy and bitters, and stir well. Add ice to fill the glass halfway, and top with club soda. Garnish with another cocktail cherry and an orange twist, and raise the glass to those in your life who have proven most dependable.

STUBBORN AS A MULE

RECALCITRANCE SOLIDIFIES ON ALL SIDES OF THE garden gate. Marianne refuses to acknowledge that Willoughby misled her about his intentions, and then she takes far too long to admit her compatibility with Colonel Brandon. Mrs. Jennings, even after learning that Willoughby and Marianne had no formal understanding, stubbornly clings to hopes for a wedding and continues to spread gossip. After Edward wins Elinor's heart, she denies herself the chance to express her love for him to others and even to herself. Meanwhile, Edward nobly adheres to his long-standing engagement to Lucy, and Colonel Brandon waits interminably for Marianne to come to her senses. In turn, each determined character relinquishes his or her predispositions and has a change of heart. A less careful reader might suspect that Austen wished to impart a lesson.

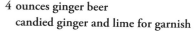

juice of half a lime
2 ounces vodka
4 ounces ginger beer
candied ginger and lime for garnish

Into a copper mug, pour the lime juice and add the squeezed fruit as well. Add the vodka, fill the mug halfway with ice, and add the ginger beer. Gently stir with a bar spoon, garnish with a piece of candied ginger and a lime wedge, and come to your senses.

"The more I know of the world, the more am I convinced that I shall never see a man whom I can really love. I require so much!"

—Marianne Dashwood

STEELE SHOOTER

LUCY STEELE'S CONFESSION TO ELINOR OF HER engagement to Edward Ferrars, Elinor's love interest, deals quite a heavy blow—just like this potent concoction. Word reaches Elinor that Miss Steele and Mr. Ferrars have married, causing heartbreak, albeit a despair borne with Elinor's signature fortitude. Soon after, however, Edward calls at Barton Cottage and explains to Elinor that Lucy has run off with his *brother*. Edward professes his love for Elinor, she joyfully accepts his proposal, and that dramatic turn of events surely calls for a drink. But drinker beware: This sweet cocktail may hit you as hard as unexpected news and leave you equally reeling.

1 ounce Barenjäger Honey Liqueur
1 ounce limoncello
1 dash pineapple juice

In a liqueur glass, pour all ingredients. Shoot it or sip it, depending on whether you are drowning heartache or celebrating new love.

THE MIDDLETON MUDDLE

IN *SENSE AND SENSIBILITY*, AUSTEN DEPICTS A FAIR amount of muddling. Lady Middleton, married to Sir John—owner of Barton Cottage, where the Dashwood women are residing—stands in the thick of it. She concerns herself chiefly with her social status and seeks to befriend anyone of importance and wealth. In the process, she and her gossip-loving mother, Mrs. Jennings, spread rumors and scandalous innuendo all about town. Meanwhile, her gregarious husband shows far more interest in socializing than social-climbing, throwing frequent parties at which he teases his guests about their possible love interests, muddling connections as well as drinks.

> 1 lime, cut into wedges
> 6 mint leaves, plus 1 sprig for garnish
> 2 ounces white rum
> ½ ounce lime-mint syrup (page 26)
> club soda
> lime and mint for garnish

In a mixing glass, muddle the lime wedges and mint leaves. Add the rum and the syrup, and stir well. Strain into a highball glass filled with ice, and top with club soda. Garnish with a lime wedge and mint sprig, and pay no attention to the rumors. After all, it's better to muddle mint than to muddle gossip.

"They met for the
sake of eating,
drinking, and
laughing together,
playing at cards, or
consequences, or any
other game that was
sufficiently noisy."

—Jane Austen, *Sense and Sensibilty*

II

PRIDE AND PREJUDICE

WHEN A WEALTHY YOUNG GENTLEMAN by the name of Mr. Bingley moves into Netherfield Park, the grand manor at the end of the lane, the lives of the Bennet sisters change forever. Bingley brings with him his best friend, the dashing and wealthy but also rather disagreeable Mr. Darcy. Miscommunication, heartache, and of course proposals ensue as all attempt to satisfy the laconic epigram that opens the novel, declaring that a rich, single man must by definition be looking to secure a marriage for himself. If you do marry into a superior class, the situation calls for sparkling wine—as do several of these cocktails.

NETHERFIELD PUNCH

FOREVER APPRECIATIVE OF A GOOD BALL, AUSTEN wrote often about the grandeur of these formal affairs, where flirting, dancing, and drinking took place, lasting until the early morning hours. At a grand ball at Netherfield, Charles Bingley would have served a punch like this. A vibrant and lively concoction, it will facilitate dancing and flirtation at your next fete.

SERVES 8–10

2 (750 ml) bottles red wine, chilled
¾ cup orange brandy
½ cup pear brandy
2 cups orange juice
¼ cup lime juice
2 cups sparkling water
lemon, lime, and orange for garnish

In a punch bowl, pitcher, or drinks dispenser, combine all liquid ingredients and add ice to fill. Garnish with thin slices of citrus, and should guests continue to mill about your home as dawn arrives, attribute it to the punch.

> "My dear Hill, have you heard the good news? Miss Lydia is going to be married; and you shall all have a bowl of punch to make merry at her wedding."
>
> —Mrs. Bennet

SHORT & LONGBOURN

THE BENNET FAMILY'S COUNTRY MANOR, LONGBOURN, is far from opulent, but the Bennet girls enjoy their lives in the only home they have known. Bitterness comes, however, during a brief visit from Lady Catherine de Bourgh, Mr. Darcy's arrogant aunt, who finds it decidedly lacking when compairing it with her own lavish estate. Lady Catherine openly criticizes both Longbourn and Mr. Darcy's romance with Elizabeth. Fortunately, Lady Catherine's efforts to prevent that romance fail in the most notable of ways. Likewise, in this drink, the bitterness of the grapefruit juice only accentuates the sweetness of its surrounding ingredients.

2 ounces Grand Marnier
2 ounces grapefruit juice
2 ounces sparkling rosé

In a shaker filled with ice, combine the Grand Marnier and the grapefruit juice and shake well. Strain into a rocks glass filled with ice, top with sparkling rosé, and hold your tongue.

SALT & PEMBERLEY

WHEN ELIZABETH, HER AUNT, AND UNCLE ARRIVE unannounced at Pemberley, Mr. Darcy's grand estate, they find art-covered walls, grand pianos, and sweeping views of the surrounding hills and countryside. Mr. Darcy's housekeeper gives the group a tour and speaks of her employer with much admiration, noting his kindness toward others and his love for his sister. Elizabeth, who once considered Mr. Darcy a very cold gentleman indeed, has a change of heart. After her visit, she realizes that perhaps she has misjudged him and entertains thoughts of becoming the mistress of the house.

　　　salt
1 ounce Aperol
1 ounce bourbon
2 ounces grapefruit juice
　　　sparkling wine
　　　grapefruit for garnish

Rim a coupe with salt, and set aside. In a shaker filled with ice, pour the Aperol, bourbon, and grapefruit juice and shake well. Strain the cocktail into the prepared coupe, and top with sparkling wine. Garnish with a grapefruit slice, and never judge a gentleman without first seeking the opinion of his housekeeper.

GIN & BENNET

MRS. BENNET IS A PRATTLING GOSSIP OF A MOTHER and a constant embarrassment to her daughters. She fails to present herself well, and her children cannot prevent her from trying to marry them all off—the focus of her every waking moment. When Jane goes to visit the the Bingleys for dinner, Mrs. Bennet refuses to let her use the carriage—despite anticipated poor weather—secretly hoping that the storm will hold Jane hostage at Netherfield. The ruse works only too well.

1½ ounces gin
½ ounce crème de violette
½ ounce lemon juice
sparkling wine
edible blossoms for garnish

In a shaker filled with ice, combine the gin, crème de violette, and lemon juice and shake well. Strain into a coupe, and top with sparkling wine. Garnish with edible blossoms, and for heaven's sake, take the carriage.

....

"'If I were as rich as Mr. Darcy,' cried a young Lucas . . .
'I should not care how proud I was. I would keep a
pack of foxhounds, and drink a bottle of wine a day.'

'Then you would drink a great deal more than you
ought,' said Mrs. Bennet; 'and if I were to see you
at it, I should take away your bottle directly.'"

—Jane Austen, *Pride and Prejudice*

....

FIZZY MISS LIZZIE

BEING QUICK-WITTED, HEADSTRONG, AND STUBBORN,
Elizabeth Bennet transforms the act of arguing her point into
an art. Never one to submit to the opinions of others simply for
the sake of preserving the peace, she is also slow to recognize
love, even when it stands before her—and looks quite dashing,
one might add. Only a sparkling wine can match the efferves-
cence of her wit.

1 ounce elderflower liqueur
1 ounce vodka
2 ounces apricot nectar
   sparkling wine

In a shaker filled with ice, pour the elderflower liqueur,
vodka, and apricot nectar and shake well. Strain into a flute,
top with sparkling wine, and stand your ground.

....

"In vain have I struggled. It will not do. My feelings
will not be repressed. You must allow me to tell
you how ardently I admire and love you."

—Mr. Darcy to Elizabeth Bennet

....

COUSIN COLLINS

THE BENNETS' POMPOUS COUSIN COLLINS, A clergyman and the heir to their home and property, comes to Longbourn, looking for a wife. After realizing that Jane, his initial choice, is not presently available, he pursues Elizabeth, but she dismisses him as a pathetic, money-seeking fool. Marrying her cousin would save her family's home, but Elizabeth declines to enter what surely would prove a life of misery. This sends the marriage-consumed Mrs. Bennet into a fury—though one imagines that a steady supply of this cocktail might see her into a better humor. Elizabeth nevertheless stands her ground, and Collins reconsiders, instead marrying Elizabeth's best friend— who might need to indulge in one or two of these herself.

1½ ounces gin
1 ounce limoncello
½ teaspoon simple syrup
1 ounce lemon juice
club soda
lemon for garnish

In a shaker filled with ice, pour the gin, limoncello, simple syrup, and lemon juice and shake well. Strain into a Collins glass filled with ice, and top with club soda. Garnish with a lemon wheel, and reconsider your options.

VARIATION For a fruitier version of this drink, substitute 1 ounce Black Trumpet Blueberry Cordial and 1 ounce St. Germain for the limoncello and simple syrup.

"From this day you must be a stranger to one of your parents. Your mother will never see you again if you do not marry Mr. Collins, and I will never see you again if you do."

—Mr. Bennet to Elizabeth

CHERRY BINGLEY

WEALTHY BACHELOR CHARLES BINGLEY MOVES into Netherfield Park and immediately finds himself taken with the young woman in the cottage down the road. The eldest of the Bennet girls, Jane represents everything one might seek in a neighbor as well as a wife: She is sweet, kind, and good-natured. Charles's sister, Caroline, and his friend, Mr. Darcy, initially do not approve of the match and attempt to separate Bingley from the object of his affections, but the two doubters appreciate soon enough that the love between Charles and Jane rings true. Perhaps that is the cherry on top.

1½ ounces cachaça
1½ ounces cherry liqueur
½ ounce lime juice
club soda
lime and cocktail cherry for garnish

In a shaker filled with ice, combine the cachaça, cherry liqueur, and lime juice. Shake well, and strain into a rocks glass filled with ice. Top with club soda, garnish with a lime wheel and a cocktail cherry, and hold steady.

NOTE For this recipe, select an unaged cachaça and a cherry liqueur such as cherry heering, maraschino, or kirsch.

WEEDING THE GARDINER

MRS. BENNET'S BROTHER, MR. GARDINER, AND his wife are possessed of intelligence, taste, and manners—in notable contrast to their ignorant and flighty sister. Having no children of their own, the Gardiners dote on the Bennet girls, especially Jane and Elizabeth, bringing them to London several times a year to attend dinners and parties and to mingle in society. For the young ladies, the kind and proper conduct of the Gardiners makes them feel as warm and comforted as this cocktail will make you feel.

- ¼ **cup heavy cream**
- ¼ **cup whole milk**
- 1 **tablespoon maple syrup**
- 1 **teaspoon caramel sauce**
- ½ **teaspoon vanilla extract**
- 1½ **ounces brandy**
- 1½ **ounces rum**
- **whipped cream, nutmeg, and cinnamon for garnish**

In a saucepan over medium heat, combine the cream, milk, maple syrup, caramel sauce, and vanilla. Stir constantly until the caramel sauce and syrup dissolve, but take care not to scald the milk. Remove from heat, and add the brandy and rum. Stir and strain into a chafed Irish coffee mug. Top with whipped cream and rasped cinnamon and nutmeg, and then make another for someone who dotes on you.

III

MANSFIELD PARK

M R. AND MRS. PRICE SEND THEIR daughter Fanny to live with her wealthy uncle and aunt, Sir Thomas and Lady Bertram, in their impressive manor at Mansfield Park. Never treated fairly, Fanny lodges in a drafty room in the attic and suffers the scorn of her cousins and decidedly cross aunt. But Fanny persists and finds solace in her friendship with Edmund, a cousin by marriage. As Fanny is coming of age, Sir Thomas sails for Antigua to review his plantations there. While he is away, Mansfield Park errupts in affairs, love triangles, immoral behavior, and other theatrics both literal and figurative. In recognition of Sir Thomas's fateful trip, many of these cocktails have a tropical flair.

PLANTATION PUNCH

THE GREAT HOUSE OF MANSFIELD PARK IS AN impressive estate indeed. To maintain such a grand property, Sir Thomas relies on income from plantations that his family owns in Antigua. This fruity concoction marries rum—such as Sir Thomas might have produced on his plantation—with other island flavors that he would have tasted there. Serve it at your next summer party or grand ball such as that thrown at Mansfield Park upon Sir Thomas's return.

SERVES 8–10

2 cups light rum
1 cup dark rum
1 cup Grand Marnier
4 cups pineapple juice
1 cup coconut nectar
1 cup orange juice
4 ounces lemon juice
2 ounces grenadine
lemon, lime, orange, pineapple, and cocktail cherries for garnish

In a punch bowl, pitcher, or drinks dispenser filled with ice, combine all liquid ingredients, add fruit slices and cherries, and mix well.

"But there certainly are not so many men of large fortune in the world as there are pretty women to deserve them."

—Jane Austen, *Mansfield Park*

"Edmund said no more to either lady; but going quietly to another table, on which the supper-tray yet remained, brought a glass of Madeira to Fanny, and obliged her to drink the greater part. She wished to be able to decline it; but the tears, which a variety of feelings created, made it easier to swallow than to speak."

—Jane Austen, *Mansfield Park*

THE PRICE OF LOVE

MISS PRICE FEELS THE COST OF MARRYING FOR MONEY is too great, and she refuses Henry Crawford's proposal because she cannot envision loving him. Her decision comes at great expense, however: Sir Thomas sends her back to Portsmouth and her former life in a house full of noise, disorder, and impropriety so that she might evaluate her choice. Doing so removes her from the elegance and luxury of Mansfield Park as well as from Edmund, her love interest who resides therein. But fate intervenes, and soon Fanny must return to Mansfield Park to care for Edmund's brother Tom, who has fallen ill from excessive carousing. Fanny again encounters Edmund, who is no longer distracted by the neighbors. He realizes Miss Price's worth to him, and the value of their mutual attachment proves, well, priceless.

1 ounce pisco
1 ounce light rum
¾ ounce cherry liqueur
¾ ounce Velvet Falernum
¾ ounce grapefruit juice
¾ ounce pineapple juice
½ ounce lime juice
    cocktail cherry for garnish

In a shaker filled with ice, combine all liquid ingredients and shake well. Strain into a coupe, garnish with a cocktail cherry, and try not to think about what love has cost you.

ANTIGUA LOVE TRIANGLE

JULIA LOVES HENRY; HENRY LOVES MARIA; MARIA is engaged to marry Rushworth. By the beginning of volume two, these romantic entanglements have changed course but have become no less complicated: Henry loves Fanny; Fanny loves Edmund; Edmund loves Mary; Mary loves Edmund but refuses to consider marrying a clergyman. While the master of the house is away in the Caribbean, the children will play—or at least attempt to put one on. This cast of characters is not wanting for drama.

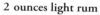

    2 ounces light rum
    2 ounces Amontillado
    2 ounces passion fruit nectar
    ½ ounce hibiscus syrup (page 25)
    edible hibiscus flower for garnish

In a shaker filled with ice, combine all liquid ingredients and shake well. Strain into a coupe, garnish with an edible hibiscus flower, and try not to find yourself in one of these triangles.

FANNY'S FOLLY

OUTGROWING HER INITIAL CHILDHOOD TIMIDNESS, Fanny Price becomes a modest, morally just, beautiful young woman. After enduring the rudeness of her aunt Norris, the demands of her aunt Bertram, and the disdain of her cousins, she finally finds love with the dashing son of Sir Thomas of Mansfield Park. After all of that, who would not have need of something light and refreshing?

SERVES 5

1 (750 ml) bottle light white wine, such as Sauvignon Blanc or Reisling
½ cup apricot brandy
½ cup peach brandy
2 ounces lemon juice
lemon, peach, mint for garnish

In a punch bowl, pitcher, or drinks dispenser filled with ice, pour the wine, brandies, and lemon juice. Chill for 20 minutes. Divide among wineglasses, and garnish each with a lemon wheel, peach slices, and a sprig of mint in the hopes of pleasing a demanding crowd.

. . . .

"Never had Fanny more wanted a cordial. . .
To-morrow! to leave Portsmouth to-morrow! She
was, she felt she was, in the greatest danger of being
exquisitely happy, while so many were miserable."

—Fanny on discovering she was returning to Mansfield Park

. . . .

NEITHER NORRIS

LADY BERTRAM'S SISTER AND FANNY'S OTHER aunt, Mrs. Norris proves herself selfish, manipulative, and frugal to a fault. Among her nieces, she favors Julia and Maria Bertram, never missing a chance to remind Fanny of her lesser place in life. Mr. Norris suffers from poor health, so he stands in no position to protect his niece from his wife's insults and demands—even if he wanted to do so. This classic cocktail, as brisk and medicinal as Lady Bertram's aromatic vinegar, is necessary after running petty errands in searing heat or when life has dealt a similarly heavy blow.

1½ ounces Campari
1½ ounces Hendricks gin
1½ ounces sweet vermouth
    orange for garnish

In a mixing glass filled with ice, combine the Campari, gin, and vermouth, stir well, and strain into a rocks glass filled with ice. Garnish with an orange twist, purse your lips, and count your blessings.

....

"Selfishness must always be forgiven, you know, because you know there is no hope of a cure."

—Miss Crawford

....

THE BUM'S RUSHWORTH

POOR, FOOLISH, SOCIALLY INEPT MR. RUSHWORTH!
He is blind to the fact that his wife, the former Maria Bertram,
constantly engages in coquetry with Henry Crawford, the
Bertrams' new neighbor. A scandalous affair ensues, and Mrs.
Rushworth runs off with Crawford; but he soon discards her,
leaving her heartbroken and alone. Mr. Rushworth secures
a divorce from her and sets his attentions on his plants and
pheasants. At least they bring him true happiness, and in the
end, such an arrangement is not the greatest of misfortunes.

> 1 ounce cognac
> 1 ounce light rum
> 1 ounce Tawny port
> ½ ounce Bénédictine
> 2 dashes grapefruit bitters
> grapefruit for garnish

In a shaker filled with ice, combine all liquid ingredients and
shake well. Strain into a rocks glass filled with ice, garnish
with a grapefruit twist, and focus on your pheasants.

"Mrs. Norris, most happy to assist in the duties of the day, by spending it at the Park to support her sister's spirits, and drinking the health of Mr. and Mrs. Rushworth in a supernumerary glass or two, was all joyous delight."

—Jane Austen, *Mansfield Park*

THE VICAR'S VESPER

IN THE END, EDMUND IS HAPPY TO PREACH THE good word as a clergyman in the vicarage at Mansfield Park. Ian Fleming gave us the "Vesper" in the martini when James Bond first ordered it in *Casino Royale*. Vicars and secret agents alike are in the business of saving souls, each in their own way, so it is fitting that they should share a cocktail. No need for separation of church and state.

3 ounces London dry gin
1 ounce vodka
½ ounce Lillet Blanc or Cocchi Americano
lemon for garnish

In a shaker filled with ice, combine all liquid ingredients and shake well. Rub a thin twist of lemon around the rim of the martini glass, and drop it in. Strain the cocktail into the glass, and say your prayers.

PEARLY YATES

WOE BETIDE THE GUEST WHO STIRS AFFAIRS IN dramatic fashion. Mr. Yates, a guest of Tom Bertram and a theater aficionado, plays just that role for the Bertram family. While Sir Thomas is away in Antigua, Yates persuades everyone—with the exception of Fanny and Edmund—to act in *Lover's Vows*, a scandalous play. Just before opening night, Sir Thomas returns home early and halts the production. Mr. Yates seeks and finds yet more drama elsewhere by eloping with Julia, Tom's younger sister.

2 ounces bourbon
1 ounce peach liqueur
4 dashes peach bitters
sparkling wine
basil for garnish

In a mixing glass filled with ice, combine the bourbon, peach liqueur, and bitters and stir, like Mr. Yates. Strain into a Collins glass filled with ice, top with sparkling wine, and garnish with a sprig of basil.

IV

EMMA

*A*USTEN CLAIMED THAT NO ONE BUT HER could love Emma Woodhouse, who fancies herself the matchmaker for the entire Highbury social scene. Emma is especially keen on finding a prospect for her friend Harriet Smith. To the detriment of all, however, Emma frequently misplaces her assumptions of love and affection, meanwhile failing to recognize the obvious connections taking place without her assistance. The patient Mr. Knightley, a close family friend, encourages Emma to overcome her injurious inclinations. When not involved in the latest social scandal, Emma spends much of her time savoring the gardens of Hartfield, her family home. These delectable drinks allude to the cottage garden there, and in them you'll find fruits, flowers, and herbs aplenty to muddle into flavorful cocktails.

NO WEYMOUTH

A CHARMING COASTAL TOWN SET ON AN IDYLLIC harbor with boats sailing in and out on the tides, Weymouth draws its fair share of visitors. Here Frank Churchill and Jane Fairfax fall in love and furtively become betrothed. Keeping their secret for months, they deceive even Emma, who has made it her life's work to know the comings and goings of everyone in Highbury—which, with her muddling, could rival the London ball circuit in terms of goings-on.

4 blackberries, plus 1 for garnish
1 sage leaf, plus 2 for garnish
1 ounce lime juice
2 ounces silver tequila
1 ounce triple sec
1 ounce pineapple juice

In a shaker, muddle the blackberries and sage with the lime juice. Add ice, tequila, triple sec, and pineapple juice, shake well, and strain into a rocks glass. Garnish with a blackberry and sage leaves, and observe the spectacle from afar.

"If I loved you less,
I might be able to
talk about it more."

—Mr. Knightley

OUT OF THE WOODHOUSE

EMMA SPENDS HER DAYS AND NIGHTS CARING FOR her elderly widowed father, Henry Woodhouse, in Hartfield, the family home. She loves him dearly of course, but the situation proves less than ideal for a young lady. She would prefer to socialize, dine out, and certainly host parties at Hartfield. Alas, she counts it her duty to play the part of attentive daughter, and so she resigns herself to a life of quiet dinners at home in the company of her father and perhaps a guest or two. Life markedly improves on the occasions when Mr. Knightley, their neighbor and family friend, joins them.

> 6 mint leaves
> 1 ounce lemon juice
> ½ ounce simple syrup
> 2 ounces Woodford Reserve bourbon
> 3 ounces black tea, unsweetened and chilled
>   mint for garnish

In a julep cup, muddle the mint with the lemon juice and simple syrup. Add the bourbon and tea, and stir. Fill with crushed ice, garnish with a mint sprig, and dream of exciting times.

OH MY GODDARD

HEADMISTRESS OF THE LOCAL SCHOOL WHERE Harriet Smith lives, Mrs. Goddard introduces Harriet to the Woodhouses, and the girls form a friendship. Harriet duly becomes Emma's diversion and protégée. Emma acts as Harriet's advisor and matchmaker, while poor Harriet becomes the unwitting object of her schemes. Vicars, Knightleys, and farmers come and go, making Harriet feel faint. Can Emma not perceive that Harriet is dreaming of love among the rhubarb?

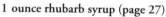

2 ounces gin
1 ounce limoncello
1 ounce rhubarb syrup (page 27)
1 dash orange bitters
   edible flowers for garnish

In a shaker filled with ice, combine all liquid ingredients, shake well, and strain into a coupe. Garnish with edible flowers, and take care to whom you introduce your friends.

"Mrs. Goddard, what say you to half a glass of wine? A small half-glass, put into a tumbler of water? I do not think it could disagree with you."

—Henry Woodhouse

STRAWBERRY FIELDS

SPRING IS A SWEET SEASON, BUT ITS FRUIT CAN TURN bitter. Mr. Knightley invites everyone for a day of strawberry picking and lunch at Donwell Abbey, his estate. The group has a picnic, which turns into a series of misunderstandings. Miss Fairfax departs suddenly without explanation. Mr. Churchill arrives late, cross from the heat. Guests wander into awkward conversations and misconstrue what they overhear. Perhaps a drink or two would have calmed everyone's disposition. This libation is perfect for warm-weather entertaining—from picnics to cocktails in the garden.

SERVES 5

1 cup elderflower liqueur
2 cups strawberries, washed, hulled, and sliced
2 ounces lime-mint syrup (page 26)
2 ounces lemon juice
1 (750 ml) bottle sparkling rosé
    strawberries and mint for garnish

Soak the strawberry slices in the elderflower liqueur for up to 1 hour. In a punch bowl, pitcher, or drinks dispenser, pour the strawberry infusion, lime-mint syrup, and lemon juice, and stir. Add ice to fill halfway, pour sparkling rosé to fill, and divide among at least 5 flutes. Garnish each flute with strawberry slices, mint, or both, and prepare to explore Donwell Abbey.

. . . .

"Come, and eat my strawberries. They are ripening fast."
—Mr. Knightley

. . . .

STRIKE IT RICHMOND

EMMA WISHES TO IMPROVE HER FRIEND HARRIET'S lot in life by matching her with someone worthy—and, in Emma's eyes, worthiness means possessing a suitable income. What else is a lady to do? Young women in Austen's day had few other options, so marrying into a higher social class and tending the castle, manor, or (ahem) cottage topped the list. Austen occasionally rebels against this convention, however. Jane Fairfax, for instance, grew up with the expectation that she would find employment as a governess in order to earn an income of her own, thereby granting herself a degree of independence, rather than relying on the presumption that she had to marry well. A good intention, certainly, except that a woman as beautiful, charming, and talented as Miss Fairfax has little need of other options.

cucumber
3 ounces Hendricks gin

2 ounces grapefruit juice
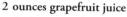
1 dash rosemary syrup (page 27)
grapefruit-flavored seltzer or soda
grapefruit for garnish

Rinse a Collins glass with water, wrap a long cucumber ribbon around the inside, and carefully add ice. In a shaker filled with ice, combine the gin, grapefruit juice, and rosemary syrup, and shake well. Strain into the prepared Collins glass, and top with the seltzer or soda. Garnish with a grapefruit wedge, and consider your options.

WHAT'S IN THE BOX HILL?

PERHAPS THE HEAT IS TO BLAME, BUT SOMETHING at Box Hill makes everyone behave badly. Emma and Mr. Churchill engage in flirtatious conversation, which leads to misunderstandings with repercussions far beyond what either party could have imagined. Emma behaves coarsely to Miss Bates, which no one finds amusing, as she had intended. Mr. Knightley reprimands Emma for her behavior, leaving her in tears on her way home. Perhaps everyone indulged in too much punch—or not quite enough.

SERVES 6

1 (750 ml) bottle Pinot Grigio
4 ounces apricot brandy
4 ounces tequila blanco
1 cup pineapple juice
lemon, lime, and orange
1 cup lemon-flavored seltzer

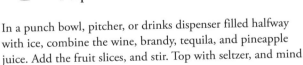

In a punch bowl, pitcher, or drinks dispenser filled halfway with ice, combine the wine, brandy, tequila, and pineapple juice. Add the fruit slices, and stir. Top with seltzer, and mind your manners.

....

"It is such happiness when good people
get together—and they always do."

—Miss Bates

....

LIFE'S NOT FAIRFAX

A WISER SOUL MIGHT ADVISE EMMA TO ABANDON her lofty imaginations, to realize that life is not always fair, and to stop letting jealousy cloud her vision. Beautiful and elegant, Jane Fairfax possesses talent and independence of spirit, a combination that leaves Emma chagrined, imagining this new arrival at Highbury as more rival than friend. The final affront to Emma's dignity comes when she learns that Frank Churchill, the focus of her flirtations, long has been engaged secretly to Jane. After some reflection, however, Emma realizes that her jealousy is in error, and the two women form a friendship.

>   2 ounces gin
>   1 ounce lavender syrup (page 25)
>   1 teaspoon lemon juice
>   sparkling rosé
>   edible lavender and mint for garnish

In a shaker filled with ice, combine the gin, lavender syrup, and lemon juice. Shake well, strain into a highball glass filled with ice, and top with sparkling rosé. Garnish with fresh lavender and mint, and serve with a straw. You may wish to make another as a peace offering to a former rival.

. . . .

"I always deserve the best treatment because
I never put up with any other."

—Emma Woodhouse

. . . .

MR. MARTIN-I

A RESPECTABLE YOUNG FARMER, ROBERT MARTIN has his heart set on Harriet, Emma's protégée, but he also has a difficult time convincing Emma that he is worthy of Harriet's affection. Perhaps it is because Emma had no hand in this love match that she deems the poor Mr. Martin an unworthy suitor. At Emma's encouragement, Harriet refuses his proposal, so he retreats to the safety his farm. It may have proven beneficial for him to take one of these libations while waiting for Harriet to acknowledge and return his affections.

> 3½ ounces gin
> ½ ounce dry vermouth
> olives and cocktail onion for garnish

In a mixing glass filled with ice, combine the gin and vermouth and stir well. Strain into a martini glass, and garnish with two olives and a cocktail onion pierced, like Mr. Martin's heart, on a cocktail spear.

VARIATION If you prefer your Martini as dirty as a day's work in the fields, add a splash of olive brine.

V

NORTHANGER
ABBEY

NOT MANY READERS REALIZE THAT, of her major works, Jane Austen wrote Northanger Abbey, a delightfully sharp satire of the gothic novel, first. In the story, the Allens, family friends of the Morlands, invite young Catherine to join them on a visit to Bath, where people frequently took the waters for restorative purposes. Catherine Morland has a passion for reading gothic novels when not attending balls and other social engagements. At one of them, she encounters the Tilney family, who invite her to stay with them at their home, the abbey of the book's title. There, Catherine's fertile imagination overcomes her, and much agitation and turmoil ensue. The imposing abbey, where ghosts and secrets seem to lurk in empty chambers and around every corner, makes a perfect setting for cocktails of a haunting nature.

CATHERINE WALLBANGER

ON ENTERING BATH'S LIVELY SOCIAL SCENE, Catherine, still young and naïve, finds herself caught unawares by the true intentions of those she meets. She befriends a duo of a semingly devious nature: John Thorpe proves overbearing and manipulative and presumes an engagement to Catherine. Thorpe's sister, Isabella, newly engaged to Catherine's brother James, begins a dalliance with a renowned scoundrel, breaking James's heart. What recourse does one have in the face of such duplicity beyond banging one's head against the wall? This concoction pays homage to the original Harvey Wallbanger, a drink made with Galliano, an herbal liqueur produced in Italy, the origin of so many of the gothic novels that Catherine reads. This version of the drink contains more bite and blood . . . orange.

2 ounces mandarin vodka
2 ounces blood orange juice
½ ounce Galliano L'Autentico
orange and cocktail cherry for garnish

In a shaker filled with ice, pour the vodka and blood orange juice and shake well. Strain into a highball glass filled with ice, and float the Galliano on top. Garnish with an orange slice and a cocktail cherry, and try not to let it go to your head.

....

"Friendship is certainly the finest balm
for the pangs of disappointed love."

—Jane Austen, *Northanger Abbey*

....

GIMLET A BREAK

AT THE PUMP ROOM, THE CENTER OF THE SOCIAL scene in Bath, Catherine meets a dashing young man named Henry Tilney. He charms her with his witty inquiries and impresses Mrs. Allen by knowing a startling amount about fabric and ladies' dresses. The encounter leaves Catherine craving a closer acquaintance with the intelligent and distinguished Mr. Tilney. There is something to be said for knowing what a lady wants.

2 ounces gin
1 ounce Rose's lime juice
lime for garnish

In a shaker filled with ice, pour the gin and lime juice and shake well. Strain into a coupe, garnish with a lime wheel, and work up the courage to talk to that dashing stranger.

VARIATION For a fresher, more restorative version of this drink, subsitute ¾ ounce fresh lime juice and ¼ ounce simple syrup for the Rose's. For a more savory rendition, try adding 1½ ounces Earl Grey syrup (page 24).

....

"I cannot speak well enough to be unintelligible."
—Catherine Morland

....

SIDE CORPSE

CATHERINE'S TIRELESS AFFECTION FOR GOTHIC novels catches a spark when Henry Tilney shares a sinister tale, suggesting that where she is staying is haunted, and describes in detail mysterious chests, violent storms, and secret vaulted rooms during their carriage ride to the abbey. She allows her fantasies to set her mind astray, but the corpse in question exists solely in her imagination. Do make certain someone else takes the reins after you have enjoyed one of these concoctions.

2 ounces gin
1½ ounces Black Trumpet Blueberry Cordial
½ ounce lemon juice
1 dash plum bitters
lemon for garnish

In a shaker filled with ice, add the gin, Black Trumpet Blueberry Cordial, lemon juice, and plum bitters, shake well, and strain into a coupe. Twist a lemon peel over the drink—in same way that Catherine's addled mind twists the truth—and drop it in.

HAND IN THE TILNEY

THE LESSON BEST LEARNED AT AN OLD, MYSTERIOUS abbey is to keep your wits about you and your hand out of the Tilney men's affairs. Indeed, an involvement with a member of the Tilney family appears decidedly hazardous for women—one ends up dead, another becomes an outcast, and a third is sent packing in the dead of night. Better to share this cocktail with someone in possesion of a brighter disposition.

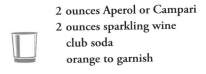

  2 ounces Aperol or Campari
  2 ounces sparkling wine
    club soda
    orange to garnish

In a rocks glass filled with ice, pour the Aperol or Campari, and top with sparkling wine. Add a splash of club soda, garnish with an orange wheel, and prepare yourself for bitterness below.

....

"You women are always thinking of men's being in liquor. Why, you do not suppose a man is overset by a bottle? I am sure of this—that if everybody was to drink their bottle a day, there would not be half the disorders in the world there are now. It would be a famous good thing for us all."

—John Thorpe

....

DARK & STORMY NIGHT

ON CATHERINE'S FIRST NIGHT VISITING THE TILNEY home, a storm rattles the abbey. Violent gusts of wind shake the windows as rain hurls against the glass. Catherine explores her bedchamber in near darkness and happens upon a mysterious cabinet that contains some kind of manuscript. Her imagination runs wild with what the document might contain—but a gust extinguishes her candle before she can read it. Terrified, she seeks refuge under the bedcovers to hide from some terrible secret that she may have discovered. Tossing and turning in the night, she imagines screams in the abbey and visitors at her door, nearly succumbing to madness. In the morning, Catherine discovers that the papers contain not depraved family secrets but an account of household linens. She had discovered—a laundry list? This cocktail will help soothe a similarly hazardous imagination.

2 ounces Gosling's Black Seal rum
3 ounces ginger beer
½ ounce lime juice
**   lime for garnish**

In a highball glass filled with ice, combine the rum, ginger beer, and lime juice. Stir well, garnish with a lime wedge, and savor the darkness.

NOTE A Dark & Stormy, by law, must contain Gosling's rum. In 1806, the final year that the Austen girls visited Bath, James Gosling departed England for America, but he settled instead in Bermuda, founding the company that bears his name to this day.

BLACK VELVET CURTAINS

GOSSIP, RUMORS, AND A FRIGHTFUL IMAGINATION torment Catherine's young mind. What dark, depraved secrets lurk in the darkness? She simply cannot keep herself away from the one forbidden part of the abbey, which she brings it upon herself to investigate. Henry Tilney discovers her on the staircase outside of his late mother's chambers. Her presence there puzzles him, and he cannot countenance that she could believe any of this foolishness. This luscious cocktail appears as cloudy and dark as Catherine's tormented imagination.

2 ounces sparkling wine
2 ounces stout beer

Fill a flute halfway with sparkling wine, top with stout, and you will find nothing more to the story.

VARIATION For an extra bump in the night, add 1 ounce of a dark and smoky scotch, such as Laphroaig or Lagavulin.

....

"If the Pearsons were not at home, I should inevitably fall a sacrifice to the arts of some fat woman who would make me drunk with small beer."

—Jane Austen to Cassandra Austen, 1796

....

DEATH BY CHOCOLATE

SPURRED BY AN UNHEALTHY PASSION FOR GOTHIC novels, Catherine believes that General Tilney, Henry's father, bears some dark responsibility for his wife's death—or perhaps he is holding her imprisoned in a remote part of the abbey. Catherine learns in due course that Mrs. Tilney died of natural causes. No foul play occurred. But Henry recoils at Catherine's preposterous theories, and she fears that she has fallen from his esteem. Rather than filling your head with the nonsense that turned Catherine into an ill-behaved house guest, fill your stomach with this libation instead. It might not kill you, but you will fall victim to its rich decadence.

2 ounces chocolate-flavored vodka
1½ ounces chocolate liqueur
1 ounce espresso, chilled
3 coffee beans for garnish

In a shaker filled with ice, pour the vodka, chocolate liqueur, and espresso. Shake until it grows as cold as General Tilney's heart. Strain into a martini glass, and garnish with the coffee beans.

GLASS HALF FULLERTON

SWIFTLY EXPELLED FROM NORTHANGER ABBEY BY General Tilney, Catherine Morland returns home to Fullerton in solitude and disgrace. She presumes that her flight of fancy about the details surrounding the death of Mrs. Tilney caused her abrupt expulsion, but she soon learns the true reason: General Tilney discovered that Catherine possesses no great fortune. No matter how regrettable the circumstances of her return, her family greets her with open arms and eager affection. The warm welcome turns an unfortunate event into something altogether more positive. Henry Tilney, upon hearing of his father's actions, soon pays a visit to Fullerton to offer both an explanation and, of course, a proposal of marriage. Catherine's glass goes from half full to overflowing with love.

½ tablespoon lavender honey
½ tablespoon warm water
2 ounces light rum
½ ounce lemon juice

In a shaker, pour the honey and warm water and stir until the honey dissolves like a bad dream. Add the rum and lemon juice, and fill the shaker with ice. Shake well, strain into a coupe glass, and raise your glass to a happy ending.

VARIATION Substitute 1 ounce Earl Grey syrup for the honey and water.

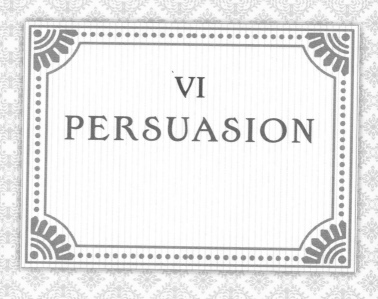

VI
PERSUASION

ON THE ADVICE OF A TRUSTED FAMILY FRIEND, Anne Elliot refuses a proposal from Frederick Wentworth. Years later, he returns from a life at sea and war and befriends Anne's brother-in-law. She then must navigate her tense relationship with Captain Wentworth, calamity on a trip to the coast, and an eager cousin's intentions of marriage. *Persuasion* at first sets love aside, holding a steady course; then love finally regains its bearings. Thank the heavens that a strong and handsome naval captain stands at the helm. These cocktails have strong legs to help you weather rough seas.

BLOODY ELLIOT

IN A TIME WHEN THE ARISTOCRACY IS DECLINING and titans of industry are becoming nouveau riche, Anne's father stands as a prime example of the traditional—and newly outdated—preoccupation with the importance of class. His taste for the finer things in life and his poor management of family funds forces the Elliots to rent their manor, however, and move to a smaller home in Bath. Bloodys are a brunch mainstay for the elite, but a few too many can lead to losing track of the family fortune. As in all things, moderation is a virtue.

salt and pepper
2½ ounces gin
4 ounces tomato juice
1 teaspoon Worcestershire sauce
1 teaspoon horseradish
2 dashes Tabasco sauce
celery, lemon, and lime for garnish

Rim a Collins glass with a mixture of salt and pepper, and set aside. In a shaker filled with ice, combine all ingredients and shake well. Strain into the prepared Collins glass, and fill with ice. Garnish with a celery stick and lime and lemon wheels.

"My idea of good company, Mr. Elliot, is the company of clever, well-informed people, who have a great deal of conversation; that is what I call good company."

—Anne Elliot

HE CAME & WENTWORTH

EIGHT YEARS AGO, ON THE POOR ADVICE OF LADY Russell, a family friend, Anne Elliot refused Frederick Wentworth's marriage proposal because he lacked fortune and title. He has returned from his voyages abroad with rank and wealth, the time-honored rewards for successfully leading his men and capturing enemy ships. He has become a most desirable bachelor—and quite dashing as well. Indeed, Anne's feelings for him remain as strong as ever and continue to strengthen during their renewed acquaintance. But can he forgive her for sending him out with the tide?

1 ounce scotch
1 ounce Heering Cherry Liqueur
1 ounce sweet vermouth
1 ounce blood orange juice
   orange for garnish

In a shaker filled with ice, combine all liquid ingredients and shake well. Strain into a martini glass, garnish with an orange wheel, and try to drown your sorrows.

YOU SIMPLY MUSGROVE

RARELY WITHOUT COMPLAINT, ANNE'S SISTER MARY—
now Mrs. Charles Musgrove—is a restless, hysterical, and inatten-
tive mother of two young boys. Anne does her duty as a responsible
and sympathetic sister by visiting and helping with her sister's daily
burdens while her father and other sister scout a new home in Bath.
While staying with the Musgroves, she learns that Captain Wentworth is coming for a visit. Perhaps she tried to calm her nerves by
sipping this warm and spicy punch, a popular drink at time.

SERVES 8

1 (750 ml) bottle red wine
1 cup Tawny port
3 cups apple cider
2 tablespoons honey
8 whole cloves
3 star anise
3 cinnamon sticks, plus 8 for garnish
1 orange, sliced
   orange for garnish

In a large saucepan over low heat, combine all liquid ingredients
and simmer for at least 15 minutes and up to an hour, allowing
the sundry flavors to marry. Remove from heat, and divide
among 8 punch glasses. Garnish each glass with a cinnamon stick
and an orange slice, and remember that duty has its rewards.

NOTE Make sure the mixture does not boil, which would burn
off the alcohol.

LYME-A-RITA

CALAMITY STRIKES IN A SEASIDE TOWN. THE
Musgrove girls decide to join Captain Wentworth on a short
visit to his friends there, bringing Anne and the rest of their
social circle. Anne befriends a couple of Captain Wentworth's
seafaring friends and imagines having been part of his life.
Louisa Musgrove flirts with Wentworth, and, while the group
goes for a walk, she theatrically leaps down a set of stairs with
the intention that he romantically catch her. Instead, she falls
and then falls unconscious, bringing an abrupt and catastrophic
end to their brief holiday. Perhaps Wentworth failed to catch
her because he wanted Anne in his arms. Make this margarita
just like the drama at Lyme: strong, salty, and on the rocks.

salt
2 ounces gin
1 ounce Cointreau
1 ounce lime juice
1 ounce pineapple juice
lime for garnish

Rim a margarita glass with salt, and set aside. In a shaker filled
with ice, pour all liquid ingredients, shake well, and strain
into the prepared margarita glass filled with ice. Garnish with
a lime wheel, and look before you leap.

LETTER HAVE IT

WHILE EAVESDROPPING ON ANNE'S CONVERSATION with Captain Harville about the nature of romantic attachment, Captain Wentworth pens a letter to her of tremendous meaning. He passionately expresses how he had loved none but her during the many years that had elapsed since she had broken his heart. "You pierce my soul, I am half agony, half hope," he writes. Echoing the captain's conflicted emotions, this cocktail is part sour, part sweet and may leave you in a similar state of turmoil.

2 ounces mezcal
¾ ounce Earl Grey syrup
1 ounce grapefruit juice
juice of half a lime
2 dashes grapefruit bitters
lime for garnish

In a shaker filled with ice, combine all liquid ingredients, shake well, and strain into a rocks glass filled with ice. Garnish with a lime wedge, and prepare to pour out your heart.

THE NAVEL CAPTAIN

AS STRONG AND COMMANDING AS CAPTAIN Wentworth and his mariner friends, this cocktail will set you on the right course—but do steer clear of rocky coastlines. Should you find yourself concerned about your navigation route, allay your worries with another sip.

1½ ounces peach schnapps
1½ ounces Grand Marnier
orange for garnish

In a shaker filled with ice, pour all liquid ingredients, shake well, and strain into a rocks glass filled with ice. Garnish with an orange slice, chart your course, and hope that your ship comes in with a strapping captain at the wheel.

VARIATION To transform this drink into a Sussex on the Beach, add 1 ounce vodka, 1 ounce cranberry juice, serve in a highball glass with ice, and hope that was sea spray.

MRS. CLAY PIGEON

THE DAUGHTER OF SIR WALTER'S LAWYER, MRS. CLAY, also happens to be his daughter Elizabeth's friend. Mrs. Clay's charms and schemes fail to win Elizabeth's esteem, nor is she alone in suspecting that Mrs. Clay might be making a shot at marrying her father for whatever remains in the family coffers. Let us hope that affairs do not sour for this gilded bunch.

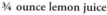

1½ ounces Pisco ABA
1 ounce simple syrup
¾ ounce lemon juice
2 dashes Angostura bitters
lemon for garnish

In a shaker filled with ice, combine all liquid ingredients and shake well. Strain into a coupe, garnish with a lemon twist, and take aim.

HURRIC-ANNE

AFTER JOYOUSLY JOINING TOGETHER, PERHAPS Captain Wentworth and Anne took a cue from Admiral and Mrs. Croft, the tenants of Kellynch Hall, and sailed together for the rest of their days. Life as a captain's wife would prove tumultuous. But with steady Captain Wentworth at the wheel, their lives are destined for smooth sailing. Enjoy this variation on an old sailors' favorite.

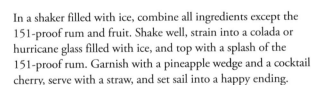

> 2 ounces dark rum
> 2 ounces light rum
> ½ ounce grenadine
> 2 ounces passionfruit juice
> 1 ounce lime juice
> 1 ounce orange juice
> 1 teaspoon superfine sugar
> 151-proof rum
> pineapple and cocktail cherry for garnish

In a shaker filled with ice, combine all ingredients except the 151-proof rum and fruit. Shake well, strain into a colada or hurricane glass filled with ice, and top with a splash of the 151-proof rum. Garnish with a pineapple wedge and a cocktail cherry, serve with a straw, and set sail into a happy ending.

. . . .

"But I hate to hear you talking so like a fine gentleman, and as if women were all fine ladies, instead of rational creatures. We none of us expect to be in smooth water all our days."

—Sophia Croft

. . . .

Jane Austen
DRINKING
GAMES

"I find many *douceurs* in being a
sort of *chaperon*, for I am put on
the sofa near the fire, and can drink
as much wine as I like."

—Jane Austen to Cassandra Austen, 1813

*Y*OUNG LADIES AND MEN OF AUSTEN'S TIME might have found the idea of a drinking game scandalous—or perhaps not; it sounds as though much debauchery took place at those all-night balls. Either way, you need not deprive yourself for the sake of authenticity. Gather friends fond of Austen and mix a batch of potent punches, such as the Netherfield Punch (page 52), Plantation Punch (page 66), Strawberry Fields (page 89), What's In the Box Hill? (page 91), or You Simply Musgrove (page 115). Then select one of the following games. You will find yourself in good spirits quite soon indeed.

WHAT WOULD JANE SAY?

Certain words and themes recur quite often in Austen's novels. On individual slips of paper, write down the following words and add your favorites:

agreeable	manner
carriage	opinion
indeed	quite
letter	should
love	sister

Place the pieces of paper in a bowl and mix them up. Have everyone draw one slip of paper from the bowl. Players take turns opening one of Austen's novels to a random page and reading a passage aloud. If you hear your word read, **sip your drink**. If the reader speaks a word or phrase with a meaning that has changed significantly over time (examples: condescending, making love, terrible), **everyone sips**. If the passage includes mention of a character's annuity, worth in pounds, or eligibility for marriage, all players must **finish their drinks**.

TWO FACTS & A FALSEHOOD

This game requires thorough knowledge of Austen's works as well as a lively imagination. Each player chooses a character from one of the novels and generates three "facts" about him or her. Two of them should be true, and one should be false but sound plausible. Each of the other players must guess which of the three statements is the lie. After everyone has had a chance to guess, those who have guessed incorrectly **must take a sip**. The player must take **one sip for each person who guessed correctly** which statement was false.

MOVING RIGHT ALONG

Many people first encounter Austen's work through the movie versions of her novels. After reading the same novel, all players should watch a movie version of the story together and drink as follows:

- A character comes galloping up or goes rushing off on horseback: **1 sip**

- A mention of marriage: **1 sip**

- A display of haughty independence: **2 sips**

- A declaration of love: **2 sips**

- A display of marriageable skills (foreign languages, playing of the piano or harp, singing, dancing, or embroidery): **2 sips**

- A proposal of marriage: **finish your drink**

- Any player exclaims, "That's not how it happened in the book!": **finish your drink and refill everyone else's**

PERFECT MATCH

Each quote below comes from one of Austen's novels. Using these and/or your own favorites, each player takes a turn reading a quote aloud and then choosing another player to name which character from which novel said it. If the guessing player is correct on both counts, he or she passes. If the player guesses the right novel but **wrong character, one sip**; the **wrong book calls for two sips**. The guessing player may choose another player to answer instead. If the second guessing player answers correctly, it's a save; if he or she gets it wrong, **everybody drinks**.

. . . .

"I wish, as well as everybody else, to
be perfectly happy; but, like everybody
else, it must be in my own way."

—Elinor Dashwood, *Sense and Sensibility*

. . . .

"The more I know of the world, the more am
I convinced that I shall never see a man whom
I can really love. I require so much!"

—Marianne Dashwood, *Sense and Sensibility*

. . . .

"In vain have I struggled. It will not do. My feelings will not be repressed. You must allow me to tell you how ardently I admire and love you."

—Mr. Darcy to Elizabeth Bennet, *Pride and Prejudice*

"A lady's imagination is very rapid; it jumps from admiration to love, from love to matrimony, in a moment."

—Mr. Darcy, *Pride and Prejudice*

"Selfishness must always be forgiven, you know, because you know there is no hope of a cure."

—Miss Crawford, *Mansfield Park*

"Give a girl an education, and introduce her properly into the world, and ten to one but she has the means of settling well, without farther expense to anybody."

—Mrs. Norris, *Mansfield Park*

"A large income is the best recipe for happiness I ever heard of."

—Mary Crawford, *Mansfield Park*

"I always deserve the best treatment
because I never put up with any other."
—Emma Woodhouse, *Emma*

"If I loved you less, I might be able
to talk about it more."
—Mr. Knightley, *Emma*

"It is such happiness when good people
get together—and they always do."
—Miss Bates, *Emma*

"One cannot have too large a party."
—Mr. Weston, *Emma*

"I cannot speak well enough to be unintelligible."
—Catherine Morland, *Northanger Abbey*

"No man is offended by another man's
admiration of the woman he loves; it is the
woman only who can make it a torment."
—Henry Tilney, *Northanger Abbey*

"The person, be it gentleman or lady, who has not pleasure in a good novel, must be intolerably stupid."

—Henry Tilney, *Northanger Abbey*

"My idea of good company, Mr. Elliot, is the company of clever, well-informed people, who have a great deal of conversation; that is what I call good company."

—Anne Elliot, *Persuasion*

"But I hate to hear you talking so like a fine gentleman, and as if women were all fine ladies, instead of rational creatures. We none of us expect to be in smooth water all our days."

—Sophia Croft, *Persuasion*

ACKNOWLEDGMENTS

SPECIAL THANKS TO ALL THAT HELPED PUT THIS book of delightful, in a modern regency kind of way, cocktails together.

Much like Jane's characters, they are all quite special and important on their own, but intertwined together in a story make for brilliant results.

To my editor James Jayo, always fabulously enthusiastic. Much like Fanny Price thought marriage to be a maneuvering business, so is the fine art of maneuvering to get a cocktail just right, let alone a cocktail book for that matter. James was the master weaver throughout the process, making sure we had the right balance of most proper Jane to lighthearted Jane, and gin to vodka, and that most importantly we all arrived to the ball on time.

To my talented photographer Chris Bain, who was focused diligently on capturing gorgeous images, setting the scene for each cocktail, making us all want to jump in and take a sip, just as Jane gave us beautiful backdrops and invited us, the reader, to become immersed in her stories.

To the art directors, Christine Heun and Elizabeth Lindy, whose creative work makes the regency period and Jane's world come to life on each page. To the sales and marketing team, and everyone at Sterling who helped in some way, a sincere thanks. To think Jane did it all with very little help, what would she do with social media and a sales team?

Thanks to Jane Austen, because without her rousing wit and prose, and immense talent of sharing stories that entertain, make us laugh, transport us to beautiful places, all centered on love, passion, and family, written with sophistication and a spirit of adventure, pushing limits of presumed and acceptable behavior, often in a funny feminist way, there would be no cocktails to celebrate the worlds she created. For that, you have my thanks and gratitude.

IMAGE CREDITS

Photographs by Christopher Bain, except backgrounds (DepositPhotos and iStock); Bridgeman Images: vi, 9, 19, 23; Lynea/Shutterstock: v; Peter Thompson / Heritage-Images / Art Resource: 6

INDEX

ABOUT THE AUTHOR

 **COLLEEN MULLANEY IS THE** author of 11 books, including *It's Five o'Clock Somewhere* and *Sparkle & Splash*. A regular contributor to Huffington Post, she has appeared on HGTV's *Insider's Garden*; in the pages of ABCNews.com, *InStyle*, MSNBC.com, *New York Daily News*, and *Woman's Day*; and as a guest on Martha Stewart Radio. She is also a featured expert for eHow with more than 70 instructional videos. She served as spokesperson for Daily's Cocktails and Mixers' "Summerology" promotion, making television and radio appearances across the country. She also was the featured lifestyle expert for Sam's Club's Memorial Day Picnic Basket campaign. Formerly the editor-in-chief of *Family Circle Homecrafts*, *FTD in Bloom*, *Jo-Ann*, and *At Home with Chris Madden* magazines, she lives in Larchmont, New York.